Lost and Found

Stories of Christmas

Through the Years...

Down through the years, I have enjoyed writing
stories about Christmas for my congregations.
At the encouragement of close friends, I have
selected for republication six of these stories that I
believe best capture the meaning of Christmas.

These stories contain tears and laughter, happy
and sad times, but within each story you will find
people who lose something and yet, through the
wondrous spirit of Christmas, find something
greater than what they lost.

I hope you enjoy reading *Lost and Found: Stories
of Christmas* as much as I enjoyed writing it.

Acknowledgements

I want to thank Joodi Archer who provides me with much assistance in every facet of writing and for being a blessing to my work; Larry Keller, my gifted brother-in-law, for his wonderful art work; Lauren Kelly for her beautiful graphic designs; Tim Mettey for keeping everything on track; my wife, Mickey Mettey, for much help with all of my books - providing editing, valuable suggestions and an eye for detail.

I dedicate this book to my grandchildren Ethan and Sidney Iery; Olivia, Cora, Noel and Ashlyn Mettey.

Lost and Found

Stories of Christmas

by Reverend Wendell E. Mettey

Table of Contents

The Little Candle

"And the star they had seen when it rose went ahead of them until it stopped over the place where the child was. When they saw the star, they were overjoyed." Matthew 2:9-10

It was a heavy and wet snow that fell that night on the steps of Old First Church. Still the faithful came as they had for over one hundred years. Their numbers were now greatly diminished and their enthusiasm was waning, but their devotion to Old First was never as strong or as courageous as it was on that Christmas Eve.

The people received tiny candles as they entered Old First. The candles would be lit in the darkened sanctuary at the conclusion of the service, as all were singing *Silent Night, Holy Night.*

Overshadowed by the large gothic sanctuary, with its beautiful stained glass windows and shiny marble floors, the faithful assembled in the first few pews. Some, however, elected to sit alone in the back where their families had sat for as long as memory served. The minister greeted the congregation with a warm and cheerful "good evening." As he invited them to stand and sing the opening hymn, *Joy to the World,* a stranger quietly entered and sat in the back unnoticed, holding his candle. Looking down as if in prayer, he seemed to be unaware of the others singing,

2

their voices now echoing throughout the nearly empty sanctuary. As quickly as he had entered, he got up and left. Pausing momentarily on the snow-covered steps, he looked at the tiny unlit candle in his hand. He threw it down in the snow and walked on.

***

Jenny would be seven in the spring. Such a wonderful time to be born. Her little brother, Johnny, was born a year ago this Christmas. He came into the world on a cold and snowy day, and his first year had not been kind to him. Perhaps with proper medical care he could get better, but medical care was expensive and the hospital was far away. But saddest of all was that this Christmas would pass, as would Johnny's first birthday, without so much as a single present celebrating the holiday or acknowledging Johnny's arrival into the world.

Jenny had asked her father about Santa Claus. Not knowing what to tell her, he said that for Santa Claus to come, they would have to have a Christmas tree. "Well, it really isn't the tree," he stammered, "but the lights upon the tree, that's it! A lighted Christmas tree is how Santa sees to come to the houses of little children."

He hurried away from Jenny into the kitchen and sat down. Burying his head in his hands, he agonized, "What a terrible thing to say to a child!"

He just couldn't tell her the truth... that he couldn't find work and there was no money... no money for the rent, for Johnny, for Christmas presents... not the littlest toy. Jenny's mother walked into the kitchen from the hallway. She leaned down and put her arms around him.

"Don't worry, we have each other," she whispered. "God has always provided for us."

That night before going to sleep, Jenny knelt beside her bed to pray. Her prayers were innocent and pure, never praying for herself but always for little Johnny, Mommy and Daddy. Lost in her prayers, she laid her head down on the bed and looked out the window of their first floor apartment at the snow falling from the darkened sky. Large flakes of snow floated into the alley that separated the apartment building where Jenny lived from Old First. Jenny's eyes followed the snowflakes to the ground. The peacefulness of their descent caused Jenny to smile and her eyes to sparkle.

Jenny lifted her head and looked intently out the window. She saw something red and green lying in the snow. Curious, Jenny rubbed a circle on the frosted windowpane. After looking back at the bedroom door, she slid the window open, scampered out into the snow, grabbed the object and then scrambled back into her room. Brushing the snow from her pajamas, she examined the object in her hand.

"It's a candle!" she exclaimed. "The kind they use in church on Christmas Eve." The candle still had the colorful red and green wax shield on it. It had never been lit.

Jenny opened her bedroom door and quietly went to the kitchen. She lit her candle by the pilot light on the stove. She grabbed a small dish as she left the kitchen. Walking ever so slowly back to her room, making sure the flame on the candle did not go out, she placed it on the window ledge, securing the candle firmly onto the dish with wax drippings. Then she knelt by the window to finished her prayers.

"Thank you, dear God, for this little candle. Please make it shine as bright as a Christmas tree filled with a thousand lights ... so Santa Claus can see it and bring Johnny a present for Christmas. Amen."

Jenny hurried into her bed next to her sleeping brother's crib, never doubting for a moment that God would hear and answer her prayers. However, Jenny didn't know that God was not the only one who heard her prayers. Mr. Ellis, the man who had thrown the candle down as he left the church, overheard Jenny's prayer through her cracked bedroom window. Standing motionless, he stared at the little candle flickering in her dark and gloomy window, his mind filled with memories of the past.

***

This was not his first Christmas Eve at Old First. He was there the year before. But then he was not alone. The person who brought him was the woman he was to marry. It was her church. It was her excitement about Old First and its ministry to the neighborhood that fascinated him so. Why would anyone so young, alive and talented find such a place appealing, he often wondered. But he never questioned her about it. She was too special to him.

To him she was a fair, delicate flower, possessing a rare beauty. He was so captivated by her; anything she did he adored, anything she asked of him he did devotedly. He came that first Christmas Eve and pretended that the church, the people and the neighborhood were as special as she thought them to be. It was a wonderful Christmas Eve. He remembered how they walked from Old First holding hands and still holding those little candles - she feeling ever so close to God, he feeling ever so close to her.

5

He now stood alone, one Christmas Eve later. She was no longer with him. They would never share another Christmas Eve again. She had died that spring and something of him had died with her. He had become cynical and bitter. In desperation he had returned to Old First hoping to relive the few precious moments he had with her that night. But the memories were painful and the little candle that he threw into the snow was something which filled him with contempt and anger. And yet he came back, looking for it! Why?

These things had been important to her and he would not do to her in death what he did not do while she lived. For her, he came back. For her, he searched the snow for the little candle. He found the candle, not in the snow, but burning in a little girl's bedroom window. And he heard the prayers of that little girl, prayers said to a God he had concluded was as dead as the person he had loved more than life.

A light crept into Jenny's room. Mr. Ellis stepped back into the shadows, away from the window. A figure walked over to Jenny... it was Jenny's mother. As she leaned down to kiss her children good-night, she noticed the flickering candle. She remembered her husband's words that she had overheard. She put her hands to her face. The light of the candle glistened in the tears streaming down her cheeks. She too prayed aloud, a mother's prayer, asking nothing for herself but only for her children. She was a mother who knew well the harsh realities of life but still hoped and believed in miracles.

Wiping away the tears she leaned down to blow out the candle. She paused. She looked upward and out the window. "Just foolishness!" she whispered as she secured the window and walked out of the room, leaving the candle burning.

Mr. Ellis stood silently in the snow. Something told him to go home. Better the little girl learn about life, about how cruel it can be and dismiss this foolishness about Santa Claus, God and miracles, he thought to himself. Yet something within him, still clinging to the belief that life was more than what was seen, held him there. He remembered how his Pauline talked about a God who works through people and how His greatest miracles were those He accomplished using His people.

"Christmas!" she had proclaimed, standing not far from the spot he now stood, "is such a miracle. Unless there were people willing to work with Him, that first Christmas would never have happened."

He was surprised at how much of what she said he still remembered. It was as if she was standing there with him. Once again he looked at the flickering candle and the shadows of the children huddled in their beds. He said to himself softly, "I'll do it! I'll do it!"

***

Gus was a favorite among the other workers. His willingness to work on holidays allowed his fellow workers to be at home with their families. While everyone wondered why Gus was willing to work holidays, no one ever asked. Confronted with such a question, he just might up and decide that he didn't want to work holidays anymore. So the others just smiled and wished Gus a Merry Christmas, as they rushed home to be with their families.

Once, Gus had a family to go home to, but that was long ago. His dear wife, Mary, had been gone for ten years. His children were all grown now with children of their own. Scattered throughout the country, they wrote occasionally and sent the usual assortment of baby pictures, graduation and wedding announcements. Gus didn't encourage them. He maintained that the cost of transportation kept them apart. Besides, young people do not want someone old around them, someone who would just get in their way.

He still missed them, especially at Christmas. Christmas! What excitement there had always been... the laughter, the little arms around his neck, the hugs and kisses. What memories. But Gus didn't want to think of those Christmases past. He worked Christmas so he wouldn't have time to think. Especially Christmas Eve... that was the worst time of all!

As Gus made his way from one part of the plant to the other, trying to blot out Christmases past by keeping busy, a pounding noise filled the empty factory. Gus paid little attention to it. "Just the wind," Gus mumbled under his breath as he continued his rounds.

The noise became louder and louder. It was someone knocking at the rear door. "I had better see who's making all that racket," he said to himself. Opening the door, its safety chain still secure, Gus asked the stranger to identify himself. It was Mr. Ellis. "I saw your lights and someone moving about. You're the first sign of life I've seen in four hours," Mr. Ellis said, shivering and snow covered.

"Four hours!" replied Gus. "You mean to say you've been out in that stuff for four hours? Are you crazy?"

"Yes. Yes, you may say that I am," Mr. Ellis said dejectedly. Gus could tell by Mr. Ellis' speech and dress that he was not the type to rob old men on Christmas Eve.

"Come on in, man, before you catch pneumonia!" Gus said as he unchained the door.

"Pull up a crate," said Gus, "and warm your hands." Gus pushed the small heater closer to Mr. Ellis. "It ain't much but it's better than being outdoors." Mr. Ellis nodded his head in agreement.

"What brings a man such as yourself out at this time of night and in such a neighborhood?" Gus inquired.

"Oh," replied Mr. Ellis, "a tiny candle and a little girl's prayers." Mr. Ellis then told Gus about Jenny and the prayers he had overheard. Gus pulled out his large red handkerchief and wiped his eyes and nose.

"This is the draftiest place," he said.

"Where can I find any toys on Christmas Eve - no, Christmas day, it's one o'clock in the morning," Mr. Ellis said, shaking his head in despair.

"You've come to the right place," replied Gus. "I think I can help you out."

"You can?" said Mr. Ellis.

"Yes, I can," said Gus confidently. "My bag full of memories will do quite nicely."

Mr. Ellis asked Gus if he really understood what he was

looking for and Gus assured him he did. Gus put on his scarf and coat. Pulling his hat down over his ears, he secured the building and turned off the lights. As he and Mr. Ellis walked into the snow, Gus said that his boss owed him some time off and had encouraged him to take his vacation time over the Christmas holidays, so this seemed like a perfect opportunity.

Gus led Mr. Ellis up and down the city's streets and alleys until they came to an apartment building. They walked down to the basement apartment where Gus unlocked the door. He turned on a lamp and told Mr. Ellis to be seated. Gus took off his hat, loosened his scarf and pulled a kitchen chair over to a closet. Reaching up high into the closet he pulled out a large, lumpy bag, tied neatly at the top with a red velvet ribbon.

Gus placed it at his feet as he sat on the sofa. He looked down at it. Tears came to his eyes as he untied the ribbon. He said that for thirty years the ribbon had never been untied. He pulled the bag down around the contents inside. There, cushioned by the bag, was an assortment of toys.

One by one, when his children outgrew them, he repaired their favorite toys and put them into the bag. He had intended to display them somewhere in the house when all his children were grown. They would be wonderful memories for him and his wife. But then she died and, deprived of sharing the autumn years with her, he kept the toys bundled up, not wanting to have such memories alone. He had been tempted on several occasions to send them to his grandchildren but something inside of him urged him to keep them. "Here is the answer to a little girl's prayer," he said confidently.

Mr. Ellis asked Gus if he really wanted to part with something as precious and irreplaceable as these toys. Gus assured him it was the right thing to do. The two stood up and began preparing themselves to go back out into the snow. Mr. Ellis looked at his watch and expressed concern about getting back in time. It was now 3:00 a.m. Soon it would be light. Gus said, as he swung the bag over his shoulder, "Don't worry. I have a friend who will drive us."

"At 3:00 a.m.! He must be a good friend," responded Mr. Ellis.

"Yes, a very good friend, a good friend to many," replied Gus. "Don't worry, he's up most nights anyway."

***

They left Gus's apartment, traveling a number of blocks through the blinding snow. At last they came to a little storefront mission. Mr. Ellis doubtfully inquired as to whether Gus's friend, or indeed anyone, lived there.

"Yes," replied Gus, "He lives here. This is his life."

Opening the door, they entered. There before them was a room full of people sleeping everywhere; on cots, on the floor, huddled in the corner, poorly dressed, unshaven and unclean. Walking past these poor souls, the two came into another room. It resembled a chapel. Finally, they walked into a kitchen where the aroma of coffee and vegetable soup filled the air. A few people were sitting at a table. They didn't look up. One person turned to look at the visitors. He wore an apron and was serving those seated.

When he spotted Gus, his face lit up. "Gus, my old friend," he exclaimed. He walked directly to Gus and gave him a big hug. Gus introduced Mr. Ellis, saying that they had known each other only a short while. The reason they were at the mission had to do with a tiny candle and a little girl's prayers.

Bob was intrigued. He called over his assistant and motioned for him to serve the tables. He invited the two men into a little room. It was the room in which he lived.

"Sit down," he said, "and tell me more about this business of a tiny candle and a little girl's prayer."

Bob listened with great interest as the two told him about what that night had held for them. Bob was noticeably moved by their story. When they concluded, he asked how he could be of assistance. Gus said they needed transportation back to the little girl's apartment.

"The mission still has that old station wagon, doesn't it?" Gus asked. Bob sat quietly staring at the floor.

Puzzled, Gus asked again, "The car, you still have it?"

"Oh, that's no problem," replied Bob quietly. He sighed and shook his head. Looking up with an apologetic smile, he explained, "Some of these poor souls have been in and out of this mission hundreds of times. To many, this is their home. Most eventually die in some alley or in the general hospital. It's difficult to give all you have in pursuit of your belief that you can make a difference in the lives of others yet nothing... nothing can be seen. No results. Each night I question why I am still here? At first, my faith kept me here... now, where else could I go?

One of the few... the very few I was able to lead to recovery is my assistant, Philip, who has now been working faithfully with me these past twenty years. But that is one person... one soul in all these years that I am sure I have helped. It just seems hopeless... now, all I am trying to do is make their hopelessness more bearable until... until it... well... until their lives end."

Gus noted with sorrow that Bob's life-long work had caused within him feelings of emptiness and despair, much like Jenny's parents must feel. But now, a little girl's prayer had reawakened within Bob his feelings from so long ago. How he had prayed for others. How he had been sure he could help make a change. Now, he did not pray any more, but suddenly, he had a chance to make a difference... to help answer a little girl's prayer.

"I want to do more than drive you there with your bag of toys, Gus. I want to give a gift!" he said. "Stay here, I'll be right back!"

Bob slipped out of the room and up the stairs to the second floor. He walked over to a desk, old and marred. He opened the top drawer and pulled loose a key taped to the top of the drawer. He came back down the stairs clutching the key in his hand. "I've got it," he declared to his two puzzled guests. Reaching high up onto a shelf in the closet, he pulled down a bag, dusty and ragged. Sitting down, he placed it on his lap. He reached inside and pulled out a metal box. He held it up for all to see.

"Many years ago, one of the men who stayed at the mission gave this to me. He was so thankful for the mission and the care and love it gave to him. Before he died, he gave this box and its key to me with the simple instructions that it

was only to be opened and the contents used when it would
help God answer someone's prayer. I'd... I'd forgotten
it was here until now." His eyes filled with tears and he
stopped speaking.

Just before, Bob had spoken of the hopelessness of it all.
Now, confronted with the box and the instructions for
its use, he was also confronted with the fact that it had
never been opened. Why? Because he had never needed
it! Everything he had asked for, God had given him. All
those men who had passed through his doors, cold, hungry,
desperate... men who had died in alleys, their lives never
changed, or so he thought. Bob had asked God to be able to
care for these men and for thirty years the doors had stayed
open, the light and heat bills had been paid and a pot of
nourishing vegetable soup had been continuously bubbling
on the stove. That had been Bob's prayer, and the prayer of
the men who came to him, and it had been answered.

But what of the hopelessness of these men's unchanged
lives? And yet, who was to say their lives were unchanged?
With whose eyes did one truly see the changes in men? It
is God who sees the true changes, the changes that matter.
Bob was there to care for their physical needs and God,
using Bob's example of loving care, sought to change their
lives. Bob wiped his eyes and said, "The contents of this
box will be my gift."

Bob took the key and opened the box. Its contents: five
gold coins and a piece of paper. Bob unfolded the paper and
read aloud these words:

> "*As this box and its contents were given to me, I
> now give them to another. I was to use the coins
> in the event God did not answer my prayers. To*

*my life's end, when upon hard times, a friend took
me in and gave me shelter and food. God answers
prayers."*

"This man never spoke much about his faith or beliefs,"
Bob said slowly. "I just assumed that a man who passed
through these doors suffered not only physical deprivation
but also spiritual. Think of it! To feel that a cot and a bowl
of vegetable soup were the answer to his prayer. We tend to
measure a person's standing with God by his importance in
life, but this man had a deeper faith than most who live in
comfort."

Gus reached into the box and took out the gold coins.
He looked at them closely. "These coins are old and they
appear to be gold. They would seem to be of great value,"
Gus said, handing them to Bob. "You could do many things
for the mission with these coins. Do you truly want to give
them away?"

"Yes," he said, nodding his head and putting the coins back
in the box. "These coins will be my gift to the little girl and
to her family!"

Bob turned the note over and wrote something on it. He
placed the note and the coins back in the box. He closed the
lid, locked it once again and left the key in the lock.

"This will be my gift!" he said determinedly. "I have no
need of it - God has always answered my prayers and I'm
confident he will continue to do so."

***

Then, the three men bundled up and went on their journey
to find the little girl and help God answer her prayer.

The snow which had begun to fall the morning of Christmas Eve had now turned into a blinding blizzard. The men quickly agreed that it was not a good idea to try driving the old station wagon in such a storm and decided to walk. The three, carrying their gifts, tried desperately to make their way in the snow. The street signs were covered with ice and even familiar landmarks had disappeared, buried in the deep drifts.

The only thing that was visible to give them some indication as to where they should go was an occasional neon sign… *"Ted's Diner - Good Food"… "Betty's Dry Cleaning."* Finally, there came a clear light shining through the snow, high over the buildings that shadowed the streets they were traveling. They wondered what it was.

"I know, let's follow it. It has to be the light in the steeple of Old First," said Gus. "The steeple is the highest point in that section of the city."

"Yes, it is Old First," exclaimed Mr. Ellis. "Follow the light, Bob."

With a surge of renewed strength, they pushed on, hoping to complete their journey before daybreak.

At last they stood before Old First and the entrance to the alley. Cold and covered with snow, they looked up at the steeple and gasped in amazement.

"The steeple doesn't have a light," said Gus.

"That's right," replied Bob. "I just remembered. It hasn't worked in twenty years!" They turned their heads looking for the source of their guiding light and there, twinkling through the cracked window, was the tiny candle.

Quickly they crossed to Jenny's apartment. Brushing the snow from their clothing, they knocked quietly on the door.

A light came on and soon there was a voice from the other side, a man's voice inquiring, "Who is it?" They stood speechless. How could they answer such a question?

Finally, Mr. Ellis spoke up. "We've come in the snow and have something for Jenny and the baby."

The door opened a crack and two eyes looked over the three men standing in the hallway. The voice again asked, "Who are you?"

"Can we come in? We have some Christmas presents for the children," said Mr. Ellis.

"Are you from the church?" asked the father.

The three looked at one another, smiled and Mr. Ellis said, "I guess you could say that." Jenny's father slowly opened the door.

They walked in and could see the children sleeping peacefully in the next room, which was lit only by the little candle. They took off their hats and loosened their coats. Reverently, they walked to the door of the bedroom. The children were curled up tightly under their blankets. The three men looked at the flickering candle. Bowing their heads, they reflected silently upon the meaning this night had for each of them.

Gus and Bob took their gifts and quietly placed them at the bottom of the children's beds… the bag of toys, the box of gold coins. Without a word, Mr. Ellis reached into his vest pocket and pulled from it a beautiful diamond ring, the ring he would have given Pauline on their wedding day. A ring she would never wear. He stared at it for a long moment, tears glimmering unshed in his eyes.

He reached out and handed the ring to Jenny's mom. "For the children," he whispered. He smiled. He thought how happy she would be that even in death, she was still helping the people she cared so much about in life. Now, Jenny's little brother could get the medical treatment he needed.

Jenny's parents stood amazed, taking in the scene unfolding before their eyes. The men turned around quietly and left the apartment as quickly as they had come. They walked out of the building and stood in front of Old First. The snow had stopped and the sun was peeking between the clouds. Christmas day would be cold but sunny.

The three men looked at one another. It would be a night they would never forget. They said goodbye and each went his separate way.

Still flickering in the window was the candle. The little candle that had miraculously lasted throughout the night yielded to the light of day. Its light quietly went out as it dissolved into the dish of wax. It had completed its task. It had guided the three to the Babe.

"On coming to the house, they saw the child with His mother Mary, and they bowed down and worshiped Him. Then they opened their treasures and presented Him with gifts of gold, frankincense and myrrh."
Matthew 2:11

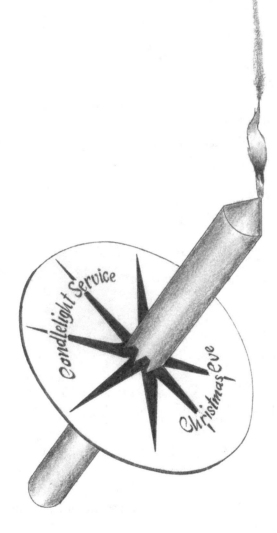

An Empty Manger

The old shopkeeper looked down at the three children from behind his counter. Shaking his head, he said, "I am sorry. I sold the last one just this morning. Perhaps another shop down…"

"No," interrupted the father. "We have tried everywhere. You were our last hope!"

"I am truly sorry," said the shopkeeper as he patted little Timmy on the head. "Maybe next year I'll have more. Next Christmas."

Walking from the shop into the cold December air, Clare snapped at little Timmy as the bell hanging on the shop's door rang out in sympathy with their disappointment. "Next Christmas! It's all your fault. If you hadn't been playing with it, it wouldn't have gotten broken."

Timmy rubbed his eyes and began crying. "I didn't mean to break it!"

Father knelt down and put his arms around Timmy. "Don't cry. We know you didn't mean for it to break."

"I'm sorry, Timmy," added Clare as she laid her head on

Father's shoulder near his. "I know you didn't mean for it to break."

"What are we going to do, Dad?" asked Aaron. "It won't be Christmas without it."

"Well," replied Father as he hoisted little Timmy onto his shoulders, "let's go home and talk it over with Mom. Come on. Let's see who can run the fastest!"

Away they ran towards home, forgetting for a brief moment their problem, which if left unsolved could, as Clare would say, "Simply ruin Christmas!"

After the evening meal, they all gathered around the Christmas tree for a family discussion about this crisis threatening Christmas.

"What are we going to do?" questioned Aaron again, shaking his head.

"I think we should just put it all away. What good is it now?" reasoned Clare.

"No, we can't do that, can we, Mom? It wouldn't be Christmas without it. It has always been under our tree," Aaron replied as he picked up the figure of Joseph.

"Yes," said Clare, "but we've never had an empty manger before. Look, they all look silly, standing around and staring at... at... an empty manger."

Once again, Timmy began to cry. Several days before, he had taken the figure of the Christ child and tossed it into the air. A missed catch had deposited it on the floor in many pieces.

Aaron exclaimed in an attempt to cheer Timmy up, "Hey, I know! I've got an idea. This is Christmas Eve, right? Well, Jesus wasn't born until Christmas Day, right? That's tomorrow. So the manger should be empty, right?"

"Great idea," replied Clare, unimpressed. "And what about tomorrow? Will He be there tomorrow?"

"Oh, I didn't think of that," Aaron said slowly.

"Okay, enough of our family discussion," announced

Mother. "It's getting late. So, off to bed. We'll talk about this tomorrow. Tomorrow is Christmas, you know."

***

Christmas morning came with a shout from little Timmy, "Look everyone, it's snowing! It's snowing!"

"Gee, how can you tell?" questioned Clare as she emerged from her bedroom, rubbing her eyes. "It's still dark outside."

"Get up, Dad. Come on, Mom. It's Christmas. It's Christmas!" Aaron yelled as he ran down the hallway.

Aaron was in charge of passing out the presents. He began calling out names as the family gathered around the Christmas tree. "This one's for Timmy… and this one's for Clare… and this one… Hey!" Aaron stopped passing out the presents. "Look at that!" Reaching down, he picked up the manger and held it up for everyone to see. Then he handed it to Father, hoping for some explanation.

Father took the manger and emptied the contents into his hands. First he held up an old tarnished wedding ring. He had given it to his wife when they were first married. It was all he could afford at the time. Long since replaced with a fine diamond ring, she still treasured it as one of her most precious possessions.

Next, he showed them a tiny sea shell. Grandpa had found it for Clare one summer while walking along the seashore. "If you put it to your ear and listen with your heart," he'd say, "you can hear the angels singing." Clare kept it next to her bed. As she listened to the angels, she would remember all the wonderful times she'd had with her best friend, her grandpa.

Then, Father held up an old, weather-beaten, scratched-up buckle that had belonged to Coco, Aaron's dog. He had taken it from Coco's collar when Coco died last spring. Aaron carried that old buckle around with him in his pocket wherever he went.

Next, there was a key that belonged to their old house, a small, never quite adequate house, but still Father carried that key with him. It belonged to the house that was their first home as a family and in which his children were born.

One last object remained, a marble. It was Timmy's prize "shooter," a gift from Father. It was the envy of all the other kids in the neighborhood. Timmy and his special "shooter" were unbeatable.

Each family member had come in the dark of the night and placed in the empty manger something of theirs which was of great importance to them... things that could not be replaced. They filled the empty manger with the things of this world that reminded them of the great and irreplaceable gift God gave the world that first Christmas.

Quietly they sat and stared at the things resting in the palms of Father's cupped hands. Carefully, he placed them back in the empty manger and handed it to Aaron saying, "Put this back beneath our tree, Aaron ... our manger is empty no longer."

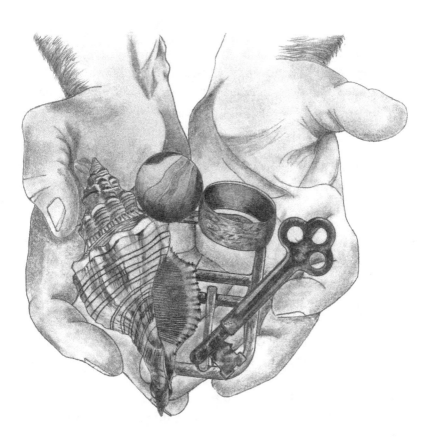

Sister Frances

It was a time of unbridled optimism. It was called the decade of the New Era. President Herbert Hoover announced to the American people that poverty would soon be no more. It was Christmas Eve, 1929.

The decade of bobbed hair, installment loans and pole sitting was coming to an end. Soon, the year that brought the Roaring Twenties to a screeching halt would be over. Two months before, almost to the day, panic swept Wall Street as the Boom Decade went Bust. The stock market crash on Black Monday was heard around the world.

That Christmas, everyone hoped this was only a temporary setback and that the Decade of the Thirties would usher in a New Era of prosperity, but few believed it. The country was slipping fast into the deepest depression in its history and nothing or nobody could stop it.

Pastors from their pulpits thundered denunciation of the sins of the Twenties and prophesied that the nation would reap a bitter harvest for years to come. Newspapers carried story after story of the nation's economic demise and the plight of its citizens. They echoed the soundings of the nation's pulpits, even using some of their theological language. America would have to pay and pay dearly for its sins of materialistic indulgence: easy credit, foolhardy spending, and reckless living.

***

John just shook his head as he scanned the evening newspaper. While the newspaper reported in great detail the sensational stories of multi-million dollar losses and massive corporation bankruptcies, John was only concerned about keeping the doors of the church building open and caring for the people devastated by the times.

"Hi, dear, when did you get home?" Frances asked as she kissed John on the forehead. "You feel a little warm. Are you all right?"

"Yes, I feel fine," said John, still occupied with the newspaper. "Really, I'm okay," he repeated, shrugging off Frances' concern.

"Do you have to go out again tonight?" she asked. "It's Christmas Eve."

"Yes, tonight," he replied. "Christmas Eve...huh! I guess it is. Doesn't seem like Christmas Eve. We've called a special meeting of the Relief Committee. We are expecting 500 people for dinner tomorrow. I hope we have enough food."

"Oh, you will," Frances said, turning off the stove. John sat down and tossed the newspaper on the table. "I don't know, Fanny. It's tough enough keeping the church doors open... and now there are so many who need our help..."

"That's what the church is supposed to do," replied

Frances. "Keep its doors open for people in need. And as long as we keep our doors open to the needy, God will never allow them to be closed." She paused, smiling. "I think I heard that in a sermon recently."

"Fanny, we've got folks in tattered $100 suits standing in line for help," said John.

"It's touching everyone, isn't it, John. The things of this world can desert you in an awful hurry. But don't worry, John, God will always provide for our every need if we trust in Him." She placed a bowl of beans and a plate of bread on the table. John looked at the meager meal and shook his head.

Frances leaned over. "Are you making fun of my cooking, John Sullivan? Look closely, there's ham in with those beans." They both leaned forward to get a better look.

"Well, it's in there somewhere," she said.

They both began to laugh. John pulled Frances down onto his lap and wrapped his arms around her. "Fanny, you are the greatest."

And you're not so bad yourself," she replied.

***

Following the Christmas morning worship, John went directly home. Frances stayed back to help prepare food for the needy, who had already begun lining up at the front door.

"John works until he drops. It's not like him to leave," thought Frances as she worked around the kitchen. Taking off her apron, she excused herself and went home.

When she arrived, she found John in bed with a high fever. John finally admitted that he was not all right and gave in to her insistence that she telephone Doc Potter.

 While Frances was out of the room, John remembered noticing a visitor at worship he had never seen before. When he passed through the line he complimented John on the service and placed an envelope in his hand. "Now, what did I do with that envelope?" John thought, looking around the room. "Ah, yes, I put it in my Bible. Now, where is my Bible? Probably downstairs…no, there it is," he said in a quivering voice. He reached over to a nearby chair, pushed his clothes aside, and picked it up.

He was so weak he fell back into bed, his Bible coming to rest on his chest. After a few minutes, he opened it and out fell an envelope. Inside was a card and when he opened it, a brand new $100 bill fell out. Reading the card to himself, he murmured, "Well, I'll be, '*Help someone as someone once helped me.*'" That was it, no name or return address.

John smiled and said with all the breath inside him, "Praise God. This will feed a lot of people. Fanny was right."

At that moment, Frances and Doc Potter entered the room. "What's all that praising the Lord about?" Frances asked as they walked towards John.

"Hi, Doc," said John. "I am really sorry to bother you on Christmas."

"I've already delivered a baby, stitched up little Bobby Hood's lip (a present from his brother, don't you know), and made my hospital rounds. Besides, Pastor, you're never a bother," said Doc Potter, putting his bag down.

"Fanny, I've got great news," John said, beginning to cough.

Frances picked up the Bible, snapping it shut around the envelope and its contents, not noticing the $100 bill.

"I didn't bring Doc Potter here for you to preach to him," she kidded. She put the Bible down on a nearby box of books.

"But Fanny," coughed John, still trying to tell her about the money, "I want you to see..."

"No, I want Doc Potter to see you," she interrupted. John didn't have the strength to pursue his conversation. He settled back in bed, thinking he'd tell Fanny later. "Nice of you to come, Doc. It's just a bad cold."

After Doc Potter examined John and visited a while with his favorite pastor and his wife, he and Frances went into the hall. "Frances, I think this is pneumonia!"

"Oh, no," sighed Frances.

"I think this has been going on for some time. Hasn't he complained... no, you don't have to answer. Sometimes courage and stubbornness are hard to tell apart. I've been treating this all over town and it's difficult to cure. It can be nasty." He reached into his bag and said, "Here, give him these pills every four hours. A lot of fluids, aspirin to keep the fever down and bed rest, Frances. Under no circumstances does he get out of that bed for ten days."

"Ten days?" she replied. "John?"

"Frances, this can be serious. We don't want anything to happen to him. We need him and you, Frances, now more than ever, the way things are going."

"I understand," said Frances slowly, opening the front door. "Good night."

"Good night. Remember, bed rest!"

Frances closed the door and leaned against it. "We don't ... I don't want anything to happen to him," she whispered as she wiped her eyes.

***

Several hours later the doorbell rang. Frances looked out the window. "Oh, it's Henry," she said, walking to the front door. "What does he want ... oh, yes."

"Come in, Henry. It's getting colder." She quickly shut the door.

"It sure is," replied Henry, loosening his scarf. "They say there's gonna be snow tonight."

"How's the food holding up?" she asked.

"Fine, fine. Frances, how's Pastor doing?"

"Oh, he's doing ..." Frances paused. "He's not doing very well," she said, steadying herself against the table.

"There, there," said Henry, putting his arm around her. "Everybody's praying for him. God needs men like John. We need him especially now. We love both of you very much."

"We know," said Frances, patting Henry's arm. "Did you come for the books?" she asked, trying to regain her composure.

"Yes. I hate to impose, but that book dealer is insisting that he get them today. Frances, it doesn't seem right for Pastor to sell his collection of books."

"You know John. He would say it wasn't right to have something so valuable when there are people begging in the streets."

"I know, I know," replied Henry. "But those books have been in his family for generations. The dealer said that if they are all we say they are, why, they would be worth one thousand dollars. One thousand dollars, Frances!"

"Just wait here, Henry. I'll get them. This is what he wants to do."

Frances walked up the stairs and into their darkened bedroom. John was sleeping. Guided by the light in the hall, Frances went over and picked up the box of books. As she did so, John's Bible slipped down between two of the books.

"Henry, can you come and help me?" Frances whispered from the top of the stairs. "This is a little heavy for me."

Henry ran up the stairs. "Here, Frances, I have it. I have it," he said, taking the box from her.

Walking to the front door, Henry kept asking, "Are you sure? Are you sure we're doing the right thing?"

Frances opened the door. "Yes, I'm sure. John wants it this way. Good-bye, Henry."

"Good-bye, Frances. I'll bring the money right over."

Frances leaned against the closed door. "Please, God, no more talk about doing without John," she prayed. She walked up the stairs and into the bedroom.

***

Elliot had been walking the streets all day. A few weeks ago, the doormen of all the fancy hotels and restaurants recognized this young man and always said an enthusiastic "thank you" when he tipped them with a new $100 bill. Now they said to him what they said to all the homeless beggars, "Move on!"

The only child of immigrant parents, Elliot had come to know the children of the privileged class at college. Instead of pursuing medicine as his parents had dreamed and worked for, he went to Wall Street. Knowing the right people and being one of the "insiders", he made a fortune. Life was easy and fast. It also became a nightmare. In one day, his paper fortune disintegrated and he was left with only the clothes he was wearing. He had too much pride to beg or ask a favor and too much shame to go home.

Elliot shivered and turned up his collar. He looked skyward and blinked as the flakes of what would be the first heavy snowfall of the year began drifting onto his face. Several hours later, the snow now ankle deep, Elliot found himself standing in a line outside First Church. Trying to keep warm, he blew on his hands and shifted his weight as he rocked back and forth.

Once inside, he turned down his collar, took out his monogrammed handkerchief and wiped the snow from his hair. The room was full of people huddled around tables, eating hot soup and bread. Church folks walked among the people, smiling and pouring coffee. Elliot wondered how they could be so cheerful at such a lousy time. He also wondered why they would be willing to share their food when, by the look of their clothes, they weren't much better off than the people they were serving.

Elliot took his soup and bread and went out into the hall. He didn't feel like being social and he surely didn't want the church folks telling him that God loved him. Sitting on a step, he heard voices. They were coming from the room a few feet away and speaking a language he knew well.

"I can't sell you these books for that price," protested Henry. "That's not the price you quoted Pastor and these books are everything he told you they were!"

"I am the only one in any position to buy them," the book dealer insisted. "My client will only go so high. I can't go any higher!"

Elliot walked into the room unnoticed. After examining the books in question, Elliot said, "Twelve hundred dollars."

Turning to see who had interrupted them, the book dealer said, "Who is this?"

"I don't know," replied Henry, walking over and taking the book from Elliot's hand. "Who are you?"

"Just another ex-millionaire. The streets are full of them," the dealer scoffed.

"That may be true," replied Elliot, staring the dealer in the eye, "but I know something valuable when I see it and I also know when someone is putting up a bluff." Turning to Henry, he asked, "How much is his offer?"

"Six hundred dollars. He told Pastor he'd give one thousand dollars and now he's changing his mind," Henry complained.

"Take it or leave it," said the dealer. "Where's my coat? It's Christmas day, you know, and I'd like to spend a little of it with my family."

Elliot walked over to the phone. After cranking it, he said, "Operator, please connect me with CH985... Hello, this is Elliot Frank. I'd like to speak to Grant and I need to talk with him now... Yes, I'll hold... Hi, G.R.... Okay. It's been a little tough but I'll make it... G.R., I have some books on Lincoln I think you'd like to add to your collection... Yes, first rate. Twelve hundred dollars, I'd say."

The dealer hurried over to Henry and counted out $1,200

onto the table. He quickly picked up the books and, spotting John's Bible among them, took it out and walked over to Elliot. "Here, Mr. Big Shot. People like you need something like this. God's big with beggars like you," he said angrily as he stormed out of the office with his books.

Henry picked up the money and began dancing around the room. "Twelve hundred dollars! Twelve hundred dollars! Wait 'til Pastor sees all of this money. He'll be so happy!" Henry stopped. He was getting dizzy. Then he remembered Elliot.

"Oh, I'm sorry... Elliot? Elliot Frank, is it?" he said, walking over to him. "I apologize. You've been so kind, I should have allowed your friend to buy them."

"Friend!" responded Elliot. "Friends come and go. Right now, none are coming and all are going." He handed the receiver to Henry, stuffed the Bible in his pocket and walked from the room. Henry held the receiver up to his ear and there was nothing but silence.

"I'll be – he called the bluff with a bluff." Henry put on his coat and left the church building. He was on his way to tell John and Frances the good news.

***

Elliot had nowhere to go and that was exactly where he was going, nowhere. His feet were soaked, his hands were numb and he was so very tired. He eventually found shelter beneath a bridge. He found a piece of cardboard and put it down for his mattress. He took off his coat and tried to cover himself with it. He laid his head down and looked out

at the brightly colored city lights reflected in the river.
He watched the snow fall, drifting past the streetlight
overhead and felt so terribly alone, thinking he would
surely die before the night was over. Tears filled his
eyes and ran down his cheeks as he prayed. He couldn't
remember the last time he had prayed or cried. "Oh, God,
don't let this be the end. Tell me what I am to do. Don't let
me die a beggar…"

Elliot saw something in the snow. He sat up. "It's a book,"
he thought as he reached out and picked it up. "It's a Bible.
What in the world… oh yeah... the book dealer. It must
have fallen out of my pocket when I took off my coat."

Elliot opened it and his eyes fell on these words, *"Let
not your hearts be troubled, believe in God, believe also
in me."* He repeated those words again and again. "John
14:1," he whispered. Elliot held the Bible up to the light
and the envelope fell out. Elliot picked it up and there was
the card and the new $100 bill. He read the card, **"Help
someone as someone helped me."**

Elliot sat, frozen in disbelief. He stood up and put on his
coat. Sticking the money and the card back into the Bible
he walked from beneath the bridge saying, "Thank you,
Lord. Now, I've got someplace to go."

***

When Henry arrived at the Pastor's house, he noticed Doc
Potter's car. "What are you doing here?" Henry asked
Lucille, a church member who opened the door. "Come in,
Henry," she replied. He walked in and saw that the parlor
was filled with church folks just standing around. He heard

crying and folks praying.

"What's happening, Lucille?" asked Henry, sensing that he didn't want to know.

"Something terrible, Henry. Pastor John is dead."

Henry closed his eyes and stepped back. "Oh, no, sweet Jesus," he moaned. He took a deep breath and walked up to the bedroom. He quietly went over to Frances, who was sitting next to John. Doc Potter and a few of the elders stood off to the side together in silence.

"Oh, Frances, oh Frances, I'm so sorry," Henry said, wiping his eyes.

"Thank you, Henry," Frances said as she stroked John's hair with her hand. "We know he's with Jesus."

"Frances, how can this be? It can't be. He spoke to us just this morning and... and now... he can't speak to us... ever again!" Henry said sobbing. Frances rose to comfort him.

"Oh, how he loved you, Henry," she said softly.

"Frances, you know how we all loved him," replied Henry.

"Yes, I know... and he knew." Frances sat down once more beside John. Straightening his clothing, she whispered, "We'll bury him by the large oak tree. The one he'd often go to when he had a problem to work out or a difficult sermon to prepare."

"Yes," said Henry, "the oak tree. He'd like that. Frances,

what shall I do with this?" Frances turned and saw the
$1,200 in Henry's hand.

"Give it to the poor," she said. "That's what he'd want. You
know what he said just before he died? He said... he said...
'Fanny, did we have enough food?" Frances fell across
John, weeping uncontrollably.

***

Frances stood motionless beside the flower-covered
casket. Mr. Hargrove, the funeral director, said he couldn't
remember any funeral having as many mourners as those
that came to John's. All were gone now except for Frances
and Henry and a few men standing to the side, leaning on
their shovels.

"Come on, Frances, we need to go so they can take care of
John." Henry gently took her arm.

"There, Henry," Frances said, pointing, "I'm going to put a
bench right there so when I come I can sit and visit."

"Yes, that will be nice, Frances," said Henry soothingly.

"It's so hard to leave him, Henry," she whispered.

"I know, Frances," responded Henry. "But you'll never
leave him, he'll always be in your heart."

Frances looked at Henry and smiled. They walked together
from the grave and down the hill to a waiting car. Halfway
down the hill, the elders from the church stepped forward.

"Frances, I know this may not be the time or place, but with the way things are going these days, time isn't something we have much of," Joseph, one of the Elders said, twisting his hat in his hands. "We've had a meeting and... and..."

"Yes, Joseph," Frances said encouragingly. "What is it?"

"Well, we are worried that if we don't find the right person to lead us, John's work... well... his work may die with him," he said. "Oh, forgive me, Frances, for saying it that way," Joseph said apologetically.

"That's all right Joseph," said Frances. "What do you want of me?"

"Frances, we want you to carry on John's work. We want you to be our pastor."

"Me? I'm no pastor. I went to seminary with John but he did the studying. Oh no, I'm no pastor. No, God called John to be pastor. I was to be his helpmate." Frances just shook her head sadly and started down the hill.

"Wait, Frances," said Percy, another elder, stepping forward. "We've talked this over and the fact remains we're in need of a pastor and we don't have one and the work has to go on; we're in hard times. And you're the best choice because you've worked right along with John and he was the best, Frances, the best. And... and... the Good Lord has called John home... and... Frances, we believe He's calling you to continue John's work," said Percy with conviction in his voice.

"Please, for John's sake and for the sake of all the needy

people he was helping us to care for," said another elder.

"Yes, for their sake, Frances," the rest said together. Frances thought for a moment and then said slowly, "All right... God help me, all right. For John's sake and for the sake of the needy. But I have two conditions: I will serve for only one year at a time - or until you get a real pastor. Each year on Christmas day we'll meet here next to John's grave. If you want me to continue, fine, but only one year at a time. If you don't, that's fine too."

"Okay," they replied.

"Second, I will not be called Pastor," she said.

"What will we call you?" Joseph asked.

Henry stepped forward and said, "We'll call her Sister Frances." They all agreed.

***

For forty-five years they met each year by John's grave and asked Sister Frances to stay on one more year. And for forty-five years she said yes - but only after arriving early, sitting on her bench, and talking it over with John. During those years, Frances went to seminary, became ordained, and gave herself completely to the ministry begun and first given life by her beloved John. She never remarried - the church and all the people who came in need were her family. She distinguished herself as one of the most dedicated and effective ministers in the area and yet she'd never allow folks to call her pastor. She'd always say, "Pastor's away; I'm just filling in." She was simply

Sister Frances. And while only a few of the elders who met
her that first winter's day were present at the forty-fifth
meeting, they always extended her a unanimous call.
She led First Church through a great Depression and a
World War; through the calm of the Fifties and the unrest
of the Sixties; and now, in her fifth decade of ministry,
she faced her biggest challenge. Unless there was a
large Christmas offering for the church that Sunday, the
community center and adjoining home for unwanted
children would be lost. The property had become too
valuable for such a use, claimed the city planners. If
the church was not able to do massive renovation to the
building, it would be condemned and razed. New, deluxe
condominiums overlooking the river would take its place.

Those dedicated to what Sister Frances was doing were
dying off and it seemed the people of the Seventies were
like the people of the Twenties; self-indulgent and not
concerned with the plight of the less fortunate.

Henry, now in his late seventies, came slowly into Sister
Frances' office. "Frances, it's time to begin the Christmas
service. There's a good crowd today."

Frances closed her Bible and stood next to her desk.
"Henry, I've searched and searched all these years and I
just can't seem to find John's Bible," she said.

"You say that every Christmas, Frances."

"I guess that's when I miss him the most," she sighed.
"We've been doing this for a long time, haven't we?"

"Yes, we have," smiled Henry.

"Do you think it's all over? Will it be there this year?"

"Yes. The envelope will be there. It has been for forty-five years," answered Henry. "Let's pray it will be there today."

"Henry," said Frances, putting her arms around him, "you've been so faithful. John loved you so much."

***

Each Christmas since the Christmas John died, there was always a card placed in the Christmas offering. And always the same note, *"Help someone as someone helped me."* With it was a sum of money, each year more than the year before, until it was a sizable amount. It made a big difference in the ministry; this year it would determine if the ministry continued.

All through the service, Frances scanned the congregation from the pulpit and Henry searched the narthex as they did each year, trying to pick out the anonymous giver. There were too many people. After the service Frances, Henry, and a few Elders waited in her office for the offering to be counted. Soon the door opened. A Trustee came in and gave Frances a slip of paper and a hug. Frances looked at it. She looked up, "Was there a card in it this year?" she asked. The young Trustee shook his head no.

"I was afraid of this," she said. "The handwriting was becoming so feeble these last years. I am sorry I never had a chance to meet this dear soul and thank him personally before he died."

Just then the door opened and Marshall, one of the older

children from the home, came in. "Sister Frances, there are two men here to see you. They look important."

"Thank you, Marshall. Please have Rachel take the children back to the house. I'll be over to see them shortly."

"I can't believe they'd come on Christmas to serve us with the papers," said Henry angrily.

"It's business. That's all it's ever been for them," Frances said as she led the Elders out of her office. There in the back of the sanctuary sat two men.

"Sister Frances," said one of the men as they rose to their feet.

"Yes, I'm Sister Frances and these men and women are the Elders of the church," replied Frances.

"Is there some place we can go?" said one of the men quietly.

"Just serve the papers," said Henry.

"Papers?" questioned the men.

"Yes, papers," repeated Henry angrily. "You're from the city, aren't you?"

"City? No, you have us confused with someone else," said one of the men. "Could we go somewhere we can talk?"

Frances led them back to her office. Two chairs were pulled up to the desk. The men sat down; the Elders gathered around the desk protectively. Sister Frances sat down across from the men.

"Sister Frances, my name is Howard Tipton and this is Austin Andress. You don't know us, but we know you. And we must say what a privilege it is to meet Sister Frances."

"Me? Privilege?" said Frances.

"Yes, you are something of a celebrity about town and you have been of special interest to our employer for almost forty-five years," stated Mr. Andress.

"Our employer was quite a wealthy man. Upon his death, we were to meet with you and give you these items." Mr. Tipton pulled a leather satchel from his briefcase. "First, this Bible." He placed it on the table.

"That's John's Bible," Frances said picking it up. "I've looked and looked for it."

Next he laid a card on the table. Yellowed with age, upon it was written these words: *"Help someone as someone helped me."*

And next, a new $100 bill, mounted in a cheap picture frame. Frances and the Elders looked puzzled.

"We also have been instructed to read you these words:

> *"Sister Frances, you don't know me but I know you and have followed closely all that you have done over these years. The night your husband died, I thought I would also. I was so low, death would*

*have been welcome. Then, in God's wonderful
Providence and Mercy, your husband's Bible and
this card and $100 bill came into my possession."*

"I remember," said Henry in an excited voice, interrupting
Mr. Tipton. "Frances, it was the man who bluffed the book
dealer. Yes, I remember - the dealer took a Bible out of the
box and gave it to him. The man was Elliot something…
Elliot Frank! That's it! And he... he... he put it into his
pocket!" In his excitement he jumped up and stood in front
of Frances.

Mr. Tipton smiled and shook his head. "You have an
unbelievable memory," he said. At this, Henry looked at
the younger Elders, smiled and sat back down. "Let me
continue," said Mr. Tipton, lifting the paper to read:

*"That night I decided to go home to my parents. I
received a welcome such as was given the prodigal
son. I went back into the business community but
for different reasons. I lived my life helping people
with the profits of my labor. I placed the Bible on
my desk, always open to John 14:1. I framed the
$100 bill so I'd see it every day. Each year I sent
someone to your Christmas service and had him
put a card and my gift in the offering basket. Now I
am at the point of dying. Having no family, after I
take care of my employees who have been with me
these many years, I am leaving all I have to help
others. To you, Sister Frances, I give these shares
of stock I purchased for $100 in 1935 as well as the
bulk of my fortune. Sister Frances, may the ministry
your husband began, which you and your people
have maintained over these years, continue to help
people like me, Elliot Frank, who only need a little*

encouragement, 'Let not your heart be troubled, believe in God. Believe also in me.' And I have.

Elliot Frank

Frances, Henry, and the Elders were speechless. The letter had taken Frances and Henry back many years. Memories came flooding into their minds.

"Sister Frances, here is the stock," said Mr. Tipton, handing her the envelope.

Frances just slipped it in the Bible. "Thank you, gentlemen. You are very kind. But all things must come to an end. Elders, I'm afraid we do not have the money to keep…"

Mr. Andress interrupted. "Sister, I don't think you understand." He took the stock from the Bible and showed it to her. "This stock is worth…" he looked around and smiled at those in the room. "This stock is worth five million dollars."

"Oh my stars," said Henry as he fell back into a chair.

"Five million… dollars?" said Frances.

"Yes," said Mr. Andress, "five million! It's all yours. Quite a nice return for $100. And don't forget, Mr. Frank is also leaving you the remainder of his vast estate, asking only that you use it on his behalf to help others." A loud cheer went up from those in the room.

"Sister Frances! Sister Frances!" Joan, one of the church members, called from the doorway. "There are two people here from the city. They said you are expecting them!"

Frances stood up. Holding John's Bible in one hand and the stock in the other she said, "Yes, but are they expecting us?!"

***

For the fiftieth time, the Elders gathered near John's grave to ask Frances to serve one more year. The ministry was now flourishing beyond belief. Buildings had been added, programs expanded, lives changed, children cared for, and countless people received hope and encouragement in the name of Jesus Christ. There was now a large staff of salaried pastors and lay leadership and a dedicated congregation. Frances could not participate as she once had. Her age and a persistent illness slowed her down. And yet, she was still needed because she was the heart and soul of everything First Church stood for.

The Elders began looking at their watches as they waited for her to conclude her time with Pastor John. This year, she was taking longer than usual. Concerned that she might be sitting too long in the cold air, they walked up the hill to meet her. Maybe this would be the year she said no to their call.

As they approached the bench where she sat, a young Elder, disturbed by her unusual stillness, ran ahead. "Sister Frances," he cried, shaking her shoulder, attempting to rouse her. "Sister Frances, wake up!"

"Oh, no," said another Elder, drawing near. "Oh, no... Sister Frances."

One by one they knelt on the snow-covered ground and offered up to God prayers of thanksgiving for her life.

Sister Frances passed from this world while sitting and visiting with Pastor, who for her, was "away" no longer. In the year of our Lord 1979, fifty years after her beloved John died, Sister Frances was buried beside him. A large crowd gathered around her casket. There were only a few now who remembered her as Pastor's wife. To most she was simply Sister Frances; the person who loved others and her Lord Jesus Christ. Upon her headstone this was engraved:

Sister Frances Sullivan
1902 – 1979
"Help someone as someone helped you"

The Greeting

Mildred believed in God, but didn't believe the things people said about Him. She didn't like church nor the people who did. Things were far more complicated, the universe too great a mystery, and life too complex for any person or book to explain. And yet each morning, she said this prayer (although she wouldn't call it such), "God, if you are there, good morning, and if you aren't, so be it."

Mildred was honorable in her dealings with people. She followed the Golden Rule; she just didn't acknowledge the Rule Giver. Many thought she believed because of the way she treated others. When they would speak to her of such things as hope and faith, she'd just smile and nod her head. She saw no purpose in discussing things that had no rational conclusions. Single, driven, demanding, shrewd, Mildred was one of the most successful business women Plainville had ever known.

***

One Christmas Eve night, Mildred sat alone in her library. She was getting older and there were few challenges left for her in life. She found herself thinking about her business and who would carry on for her. She had no family. This night, Mildred also thought about what she believed and the consequences of her beliefs. If this is all there is then she could not even hope to live on in the memories of others when she died since she had no family. All that was hers would be divided up by the courts or fought over by relatives she didn't know she had. All that she had given her entire life for, all she had believed in…Mildred sat up. *This* was all she had believed in, the things of this world.

Oh yes, Mildred did greet God every morning, but she had never really tried to find Him. And now, more than ever, she wanted to know if God really existed. In all these years, He had never returned her greeting. Soon she would leave this life and if there was a God, how would she find Him - and if, by chance, she found God, would He receive her? Mildred put on her coat and hat and walked out of her house alone to find God.

Her logical mind, which had always been her guide, kept saying, "This is ridiculous. Go home." But her heart, so long restrained and pounding with the excitement of doing something that couldn't be explained in rational terms, shouted, "Keep going. Life is more than what is seen." For once, Mildred listened to her heart.

Hours later, exhausted, cold and lost, her mind was saying smugly, "I told you so." But her heart, feeling the exhilaration of its first great faith adventure, urged her to continue.

Mildred stopped. She took a deep breath and said, "This is crazy. I surely have the courage to die the way I have lived and believed." She looked up at the sky. It was morning. She said sarcastically, "God, if you are there, good morning, and …"

"Miss Mildred, is that you?"

"God, is that you?" she gasped in a startled voice.

"Miss Mildred, is it you?" said the voice again. Mildred turned around and there was Clarence, her gardener.

"Clarence, it's you!" she said with a sigh of relief, yet somewhat disappointed.

"Miss Mildred, what are you doing out here this early in the morning?" Clarence continued.

"Oh, I was just out for a little walk," Mildred said, gaining her composure. "Clarence, please call William to come and get me."

"Miss Mildred, today is Christmas. You gave all the servants the day off, remember?" replied Clarence.

"Oh, so I did. Well, I'll just have to walk home then." Mildred thought for a moment and asked, "Clarence, why are you here?"

"This is where I live." Clarence pointed to a nearby apartment building. "The missus and I have lived up in that apartment for 35 years. We've raised four children there and they are all coming home today for Christmas."

"That's nice, Clarence. Well, if you'll point me in the right direction, I'll be going," said Mildred.

"Oh, Miss Mildred, I can't let you go alone. I'll walk you home…"

"Or until we find a taxi," finished Mildred.

Clarence just smiled and said, "Yes Ma'am."

As they walked, they talked about many things. Clarence had worked for Mildred for 25 years. She paid him well and treated him fairly, but had never had time for the important things like getting to know him.

"Clarence, do you know who I thought you were back there?" asked Mildred. Clarence shook his head no. "I thought you were God, or at least His voice."

Clarence laughed, "God? No, not me, Miss Mildred. Maybe I sometimes wish I was an angel," continued Clarence, "so I could ask God to answer you. I've prayed all these years that one day He'd return your greeting."

Mildred stopped, looking surprised. "You know about that? Who told you?" Mildred said with some anger in her voice.

"Nobody, Ma'am. You see, you've been coming to the garden each morning and saying your greeting and, Miss Mildred, I'm always there 'cause I'm your gardener," Clarence said gently.

Mildred smiled and then they both laughed. They continued their walk.

"Clarence, do you greet God?" Mildred asked.

"Yes, Ma'am," Clarence nodded.

"Does He ever greet you back?" Mildred asked again.

"Yes, Ma'am, every time," Clarence nodded again.

"How do you know? How does He greet you?"

"Well, He greets me each time a flower blooms in my garden, each morning when the sun comes up. He greets me each time I see someone being kind to someone. He greets me when my children hug my neck and my wife says 'I love you, Clarence, you're the best husband in the world.' He greets me when I read in the Good Book about Jesus and how He died for poor old Clarence. He's greeted me these past many years through you, Miss Mildred."

"Through me?" Mildred asked with a puzzled look on her face and tears in her eyes.

"Yes, Ma'am," replied Clarence. "Each day when you greet God, God greets me. He's saying, "Good morning, Clarence. Mildred needs me, so go to her and tell her how to find me."

"Yes, that's why I'm out here today. I'm trying to find Him. How do I find Him? How do I find Him, Clarence?"

Clarence looked Miss Mildred right in the eyes, his face glowing radiantly. "You find God within you, and in the lives and faces of others you reach out to." Clarence stepped back. "I must be going, Miss Mildred. You're all right now?"

Mildred cried out, "Wait, Clarence, tell me more. Take me home."

"You are home now. You know where to find Him," Clarence's voice faded away.

"Clarence, Clarence," shouted Miss Mildred.

***

"Miss Mildred, Miss Mildred, wake up…wake up."
Mildred opened her eyes and looked around. She was back
in her library. "Where is Clarence? Where is Clarence?"
she shouted.

"Miss Mildred," said Katherine, one of her maids, "you've
had a dream."

"Where's Clarence?" she said frantically.

"Why, Miss Mildred, you know Clarence died over five
years ago."

Later, she and her chauffer, William, were driving
the streets of Plainville, with Mildred giving William
directions. "Miss Mildred, how do you know these streets?
I've never taken you here before," William asked.

"There," said Mildred. "There's Clarence's house. Pull
over. Pull over."

"Yes, Ma'am," William said. *"But how does she know
where Clarence lived?"* he whispered under his breath.

Mildred got out of the car, rushed into the apartment
building and up the flight of stairs, with William right
behind her. She knocked on the apartment door. A woman
opened it. She looked at Mildred and then recognized
William.

William said, "Margaret, I don't know if you've met Miss
Mildred. She was a friend of Clarence's."

"Miss Mildred," she said, surprised.

"Yes, I'm Miss Mildred... I want to see Clarence..."
Mildred paused as Margaret began to cry. Mildred then
realized that Clarence was, indeed, gone. But it had seemed
so real.

She slowly turned towards the stairs. She paused, turned
back again and said, "Margaret, would you come to my
house and have Christmas with me?"

By that time, the entire family was gathered around the
doorway. "Oh, that is so kind, Miss Mildred. But all the
children and grandchildren are home for Christmas and I've
got a ham and fixin's cooking, and…"

"I would like all of you to come," Mildred interrupted.
"Would you do that for me and for Clarence?"

Margaret smiled, "For you and for Clarence, please come
and have Christmas with us. Clarence was the best man
who walked this earth, except, of course, our precious
Lord. He had a powerful belief in God and found God in
just about everything. Miss Mildred, before he died, he
told me one day you'd come. He had already talked it over
with the Lord." Margaret smiled as she shook her head in
amazement. "And here you are!"

Mildred looked at Clarence's family, and said, "I can see
Clarence and the God he believed in in all of you. I would
be honored to have Christmas with you."

***

The next morning Mildred stood on her patio. She looked
down and could not believe her eyes. There was her prize-

winning rosebush, brown and pruned for the winter. But there, right in the middle of the bush, was one beautiful rose. Cupping it gently in her hands she said softly, "Thank you Clarence, for helping me find God." She stood up and greeted God as she had done for so many mornings, but this time…"Good morning, God, it's wonderful to know you are there."

A gust of wind whistled through the trees overhead.

Mildred smiled. In the rush of wind she heard, "God can be found in a thankful heart, Miss Mildred."

The Bethlehem Plot

"Your Majesty, there are three astrologers from the East wishing an audience."

"Astrologers! Tell them I have my own astrologers and sorcerers and plenty of scribes. I need no further protection. Send them away."

"But your Majesty, they have come a great distance."

"A great distance! No distance is a great distance to see King Herod! Give them new sandals and send them home." Herod roared with laughter.

"...but your Majesty, they speak of the Great Star and have filled Jerusalem with rumors because of their questions, asking "Where is the newborn King of the Jews?"

Herod choked on his wine, "An infant King, the Great Star? Send them in, you fool!"

The three astrologers, showing signs of a long journey, entered the throne room and bowed low before Herod. They introduced themselves simply as Melchior, Balthasar and Gaspar, three men following the star.

"An infant King? Where?" Herod rudely interrupted.

"We are not sure," said Gaspar. "When the Great Star first appeared in the Heavens, it stood still over our country. Then it began to move and now, for five new moons, we have followed. One night, tired and discouraged, we camped near an oasis. 'Why are we following a star?' we questioned.

But that night we met a holy man who knew of the star and the prophecy concerning it: '*O little town of Bethlehem, you are not just an unimportant Judean village, for a governor shall rise from you to rule my Israel...therefore, the Lord Himself will give you a sign. 'Behold, a young woman shall conceive and bear a son and shall call his name Immanuel.'* Pointing to the Great Star, the holy man said, '*That's the sign. When it comes to rest, there you will find He who is called Emmanuel.'* At last the star came to rest over Bethlehem as promised."

"Why have you come to me?" snapped, Herod.

"We thought that the great King Herod might know where in Bethlehem the babe is to be found," said Balthazar. "Can you help us?"

"Help...help," stammered Herod, his mind racing. "Why certainly, but first some food, and drink..."

Melchior interrupted, "Your Majesty, our long trip has made us impatient. We seek to fill our souls, not our bellies!"

"Now, you wouldn't like to disappoint the King, would you?" Herod's mouth curled up in a sneer. He clapped his hands and howled, "Food and drink for my guests!"

Reluctantly, the three astrologers followed Herod's servant into an adjoining room. After they were gone, Herod assembled all the chief priests and scribes. "Is it true?" He screamed. "An infant King to be born here in my Kingdom?"

One of the chief priests, holding the sacred scroll in his hands, slowly stepped forward and hesitantly said, "So it is written, your Majesty."

Herod's face became red, his lips tightened and his eyes shifted from corner to corner. They all knew that look. Herod was plotting something monstrous. Finally, an evil smile spread across his face. He summoned his guests and said to them, "My scribes and chief priests are unable to tell me the exact location of this child. But go and search diligently for the child, and when you have found Him, bring me word, that I too may come and worship Him."

Herod then said farewell to his guests, withdrew to his bedroom and sent for the Captain of the Palace Guard. When the Captain arrived, he found Herod down on his knees, hitting the floor with his fists and screaming like a mad man, "God will not do this to me. I will not let Him. He's trying to take my throne, but I won't let Him!" Herod stopped for a moment and looked up at his Captain. He told the Captain to follow the strangers from the East and "when you find the child, kill Him and all present." The Captain saluted Herod and was off on his mission of murder.

***

Beneath Herod's window rested a blind beggar named Albathar. He loitered near the palace hoping for royal handouts. He overheard Herod's conversation, but paid little attention. He had overheard so many conversations of terror from that room that little shocked him. All he wanted to do was sleep and keep warm in the cool Judean night air.

Albathar's eyes began to burn. He sat up, rubbing them. Squinting and rubbing, he looked upward and saw a light. The more he rubbed, the brighter the light became. He stood on his feet and stared in amazement. He could see, and his first sight was of the heavens and the Great Star. He looked at his hands, arms and feet. He jumped around yelling, "I can see, I can see."

He stood back and looked at the palace wall. The trees and bushes were all just as he had imagined. He danced around and around. He became so dizzy he fell flat on his back, laughing like a man without any sense. Then he heard something. He stopped laughing and listened to the wind as it whispered through the trees, "He brings sight to the blind, E-M-M-A-N-U-E-L, E-M-M-A-N-U-E-L."

Albathar sat up and repeated what he thought he had heard, "He brings sight to the blind, Emmanuel, Emmanuel." The wind then whispered, "Slay him and all present - Emmanuel." Albathar made the connection. He jumped to his feet and rushed down the hill, shouting, "I must warn them!"

***

On the road leading into Bethlehem, Albathar overtook the visitors from the East. He knew they were the ones Herod spoke of because Herod's henchmen were trailing them. He told them who he was and what had happened to him and what he overheard Herod say to his captain. The astrologers said that an angel had appeared to them upon leaving the Palace and warned them about Herod, but they were undecided on what to do.

"What shall we do, my son?" said Melchior. "If we go and find the babe, it will mean His certain death. But we've come so far. We feel that what we have for the child is important or the star would never have led us here. What shall we do?"

"Do you know where the babe is?" questioned Albathar.

"The Angel said that He is still in the womb of His mother, who is riding on a donkey on the North road leading into the city," answered Balthasar.

"He's not yet born?" interrupted Albathar.

"No," replied Balthasar.

"That makes matters more difficult. We must act fast. Do you have a servant you can trust?" asked Albathar.

Melchior called over a servant and said, "This is Tobias. We can trust him with our very lives!"

Albathar gave Tobias instructions and sent him on his way under cover of a moonless night. Albathar turned to the others, smiling, "We'll surely have a surprise for the great King Herod." They gathered around Albathar and he explained his plan. After he finished with his instructions, he slipped silently away and the others went on their way as if nothing had happened. Herod's men followed behind.

***

Albathar entered Bethlehem as he had all his life - a begging blind man, but this time he was just pretending.

He walked into the crowded inn, which was owned by his friend Josiah and began to ask for alms. Josiah came up to Albathar and said, "Albathar, this is not good for business. You bring sadness and gloom into my place. The people are happy and want to forget their problems."

"If I had a place to stay this night, I would not need to beg or to be sad and gloomy."

"Albathar, I have no room. You heard the decree. There is not even floor space this night."

"What about the stable? There a poor beggar would find warmth and some comfort," Albathar suggested.

"Well all right," said Josiah, "if you promise not to bother the animals."

"They can see, I cannot."

Josiah sighed, "All right, all right, just for the night."

Albathar thanked Josiah and worked his way out of the crowded inn. Once outside, he ran to the road. "Where are they?" he thought impatiently. He paced back and forth like a caged animal. Finally, he could see something approaching far down the road. Up the road came three people, one riding a donkey.

"Is it them?" wondered Albathar. In the light of the Great Star he recognized Tobias and when Tobias saw it was

Albathar, he said, "These are the ones the Great Star has guided! This is Joseph and his wife, Mary."

"You have done well, finding them and bringing them to where I instructed you," said Albathar.

"It was the Great Star," Tobias said. "Whenever there was a fork in the road, the Great Star seemed to light up the path I should take, and so it led me directly to them and then us to you."

"Come, we must move quickly," said Albathar, as he took the reins of the donkey and led the special family to the stable. Tobias and Albathar went into the stable and lit candles for light. They then fixed a place in the hay for Mary.

Mary sat down on a bale of hay and held her stomach. She looked at Joseph and smiled. "It is time, my husband," she said softly.

Tobias and Albathar went outside and closed the stable doors so that Mary and Joseph could have their privacy at this most precious moment. The two men looked at the Great Star; they jumped back as if retreating from a blazing fire. A point of the Great Star reached down and touched the stable, setting it aglow. It was as though at that moment God reached down and touched His creation.

***

On the other side of Bethlehem, the three astrologers and their servants rode into the city with Herod's men right behind them. They came to a large and beautiful house.

They stopped their camels, dismounted and approached the front door carrying precious gifts in their hands. No sooner had they knocked on the door than Herod's men overtook them with drawn swords. The soldiers pushed the three men aside and rushed into the house. Instead of a babe, they found Elders of the synagogue sitting around discussing the law.

The soldiers were furious. They had been tricked! They ran from the house and seized the men from the East. In the scuffle, they discovered that the men they had been tracking were not the astrologers, but their servants dressed in their masters' fine clothes. They raised their swords in anger, ready to slay the imposters, but were stopped by the Elders' servants rushing out with their swords drawn. Outnumbered and cursing like his King, the Captain ordered his men to mount up, and off they went to face the unpleasant job of informing King Herod about what had happened.

"Heads will roll," yelled the Captain as he rode away.

***

Back at the stable, Albathar and Tobias waited for news from Joseph. Emerging from the shadows was a group of men. One of them cried out, "We did it, Albathar, we did it!" It was Melchior, Balthasar and Gaspar dressed up in shepherds' clothing, accompanied by the real shepherds who had led the men to the stable. "Your plan worked beautifully," said Gaspar.

"I see you met the shepherds I sent to see you," said Albathar as he laughed and hugged his new friends. "You don't look too bad as shepherds."

"Or you as a blind beggar who can see," quipped Melchior. They all laughed. Behind them, the stable doors opened and Joseph motioned for them to come in.

"Who is he?" asked Balthasar. "And why does he want us to go into a stable?"

"That is Joseph, the father of the infant king. Mary, the mother, is inside. And the stable, that was my idea. King Herod would never think to look in a stable for the child."

"Ingenious, Albathar, ingenious!" said Gaspar.

They slowly went into the stable, nervously fussing and straightening their clothing. Young and old, they sensed the holiness that was all about them. They moved like a flock of sheep to the center of the stable and then they saw Mary. So young, thought the astrologers, with so much responsibility.

Their eyes fell upon the child resting in a manger, wrapped in swaddling clothes. In reverence, they kneeled and bowed their heads in prayer. Never before had they felt so close to God.

Melchior steadied himself as his old bones carried his tired frame to the child. From beneath his shepherd's clothing he brought out a box of gold and laid it at the Babe's feet. Balthasar brought forth his gift of myrrh and Gaspar, frankincense. The shepherds laid bread and cheese near the Babe and the smallest shepherd boy reached out and touched the Babe's cheek and smiled at Mary. She smiled back. Albathar was so happy he cried. He had received so much from God that night although he had nothing to give the Babe. Such a glorious night.

A new day was dawning and with it came word that Herod knew of their trickery and was screaming for blood. An angel appeared to Joseph and instructed him to take his family to Egypt, far from the bloody hands of Herod. The gifts from the three astrologers would make the trip possible. They all said their farewells and departed on their separate ways…

***

The next night, Albathar stood alone on the hillside which overlooked the stable. He was thinking about the friends he had made, the Babe he had seen with his own eyes and the Great Star...the Great Star? Albathar looked up. It was fading. Albathar rubbed his eyes. They burned. Everything was fading. "Oh no," he cried, "I'm going blind again. Oh God, how could you do this to me?"

Albathar rolled in the grass, moaning at his misfortune. He felt his way to a nearby tree and there, leaning up against its trunk, he cried. What was ahead of him now? A life of begging? All his dreams, all his plans were gone as was the Great Star that took his sight with it. He sobbed and cried himself to sleep.

The first light of morning struck his face. He didn't want to open his eyes for in sleep every man is blind. He refused to open his eyes or move from his spot. But he heard a disturbing sound. Someone was crying. Such a cry, a cry of deep grief. He had heard such a cry only at the pit of the lepers. He sat up and moved towards the sound. He felt his way along until he found its source. It was someone…a woman…lying across a large rock, crying.

Grabbing her shoulder, he lifted her face and said, "Why

are you crying so?"

"Do you not know what has happened in Bethlehem?" she sobbed.

Forgetting his blindness, he replied, "Certainly, something wonderful! An infant King has been born, but that is reason to laugh, not cry. What else has happened?" He shook the woman.

"This night, King Herod has killed all the male infants in Bethlehem. Blood runs through the streets like water after a hard rain." She sat up and looked Albathar in the eyes. Seeing that he was blind, she said, "Thank God that you cannot see, for sight last night was a curse, not a blessing."

And so another prophecy came true:

> *"A voice is heard in Ramah,*
> *mourning and great weeping,*
> *Rachel weeping for her children*
> *and refusing to be comforted,*
> *because they are no more."*
> *Jeremiah 31:15*

***

Many years had passed since that eventful night. Albathar remained blind, but he was a beggar no longer. He walked from town to town, giving instead of receiving. He was blind, but instead of cursing God, he gave Him thanks. Such courage! His testimony was a tribute to God, and so many received strength because of Albathar's courage.

One day in the autumn of his life, he rested near a well just outside Jerusalem. He wiped his sweaty brow and felt for the bucket to fetch some water. His hand fell instead onto someone else's hand. He grasped the hand. It was strong, but gentle. It held Albathar's hand firmly and pulled him up off the well wall. Albathar squinted and rubbed his eyes with his free hand. His eyes burned as they had at the time of the Great Star.

Albathar could see something... a face, yes a face... a face that was becoming clearer by the moment.

When his sight was fully restored, he was staring into the eyes of a man. His eyes blazed as did the Great Star, thought Albathar. He recognized those eyes. He had seen them many years before – it was the Babe, grown into a man.

The man smiled and put his hand up to Albathar's face and brushed back the hair from his eyes.

With a voice that penetrated the soul, He whispered, "Albathar, the blind can see; the lame can walk; the sick are made well. Thanks be to God."

Albathar slowly nodded his head. "Yes indeed, the blind can see more than they ever dreamed of seeing! Thanks be to God."

Tickets

Well, the computer age finally found its way into the Pearly Gates. To most of the angels this was a welcome relief, but to some it meant more work and more headaches. Mortimer, Computer Angel I, and Sigmund, Computer Angel II, appeared at the Front Gate loaded down with record books. They plopped their loads down on a nearby table and collapsed into their chairs with a loud sigh of relief.

"Oh, for the good old days," complained Mortimer as he looked upward. "Life was so simple then. No computers, no programming, no flash drives, no hard drives, no zip drives. If I see one more *drive*, I'll ... I'll ..."

"Watch it, watch it," responded Sigmund. "Remember where you are. The last time you lost that temper of yours we were scrubbing halos for two weeks."

"Well, it's enough to rile even Old St. Pete's feathers," continued Mortimer. "Nothing's personal anymore. Since we've gone with computers, everyone's a number. Nobody's a name anymore, just 782-587. Now you tell

71

me," Mortimer continued, holding up a flash drive, "Does old Mrs. Broady look like a 728-695?"

"It's a new day, Mortimer. You can't live in the past. You just have to accept it, and that's all there is to it," replied Sigmund.

"Yeah, I suppose you're right, Sigmund. You know, I had a dream last night. Do you know what I dreamed?"

"No, Mortimer. What did you dream?"

"Well, I dreamed that I was standing at the Front Gate waiting for our first customers. One-by-one they came. But they weren't people. They were numbers: 8's and 7's and 9's. And they all started crying. 'What's the matter,' I said. 'We can't go into Heaven,' a 9 said. 'Why?' I said. Then an 8 said to me, 'You see, Heaven is a 5.' Well, Sigmund, I looked up and written over the Pearly Gates there was a number 5. I scratched my head and said, 'So what?' Then a sobbing 7 said, 'Don't you see, a 7 can't go into a 5." Mortimer began to laugh, "Get it? Get it? A 7 can't go into a 5."

"Funny, funny!" sighed Sigmund. "Come on now, let's get back to work."

"Okay, but kidding aside, Sigmund, what was wrong with the old system? Remember the Book of Life? Everybody had a page. They just passed by and old St. Pete read from the Book. Sure, the line got a little long at times, but it had that personal touch. You know what I mean."

"Hey, Mortimer, speaking of the personal touch, we just

got an e-mail from the front office. And it's got both of our names on it."

"Who's it from, Sigmund, St. Pete?"

"Higher, Mortimer!"

"Higher than St. Pete? You don't mean ...!" Both Mortimer and Sigmund stood and placed their hands over their hearts. Looking up, they paused and then Mortimer began to jump up and down with excitement. "Read it! Read it! What does it say? What does it say?"

"Wait a minute, wait a minute, Mortimer! Give me a chance. The e-mail says that we are to send 253 tickets to First Church, Commonsville, USA. And the tickets are to read: **Admit One to Heaven, December 25th**. The e-mail goes on to say that the means by which these tickets are to be given out... well, that is to be left up to the church. We are to go along and merely observe and then report back to the front office on what happens."

"Oh boy! Oh boy! Just think of it, Sigmund. A visit to Old Mother Earth. Oh boy, we need a vacation. Why, I'll get my wings pressed ... my halo cleaned... I haven't been in a vision in a long time."

"Now hold it a minute, Mortimer. The e-mail clearly states that there are to be no visions, no appearances. The tickets are to be sent through the mail and we are merely to observe, out of sight."

"Ah, nuts! Nothing's any fun anymore," complained Mortimer. "I don't even know why I'm an angel."

With those words came a loud clap of thunder. Both Mortimer and Sigmund looked up.

"Just kidding, Lord! Just kidding!"

Act II
The Board Meeting

$\mathbf{S}$igmund and Mortimer's first encounter with the people of First Church, Commonsville, USA, took place at the church's monthly Board Meeting. Business was being concluded when the two angels walked in. Angels cannot be seen by human eyes, so they wandered freely among the board members, carefully taking notes for their report.

"And that will be our Christmas Musicale for this year."

"Thank you, Miss Percy," said Mr. Winstead, the Chairman of the Board. "We are certainly looking forward to the program, as we do each year." Mr. Winstead spotted another member of the Board frantically waving his hand.

"Yes, Tom. What is it?"

"Mr. Winstead," said Tom. "The young people were wondering if this year we might sing a medley of Christmas carols. We have been working ..."

"Not in my Musicale!" interrupted Miss Percy. "We've been putting on our show for twenty-five years and not one note has been changed, nor will it ever be. You don't tamper with success." Miss Percy smiled at the pastor. "Isn't that right, Rev. Holtman?"

"Success! Ha!" grunted Mr. Fletcher. "Why don't you let the kids take part? We are always complaining about them not wanting to do anything in church. Now they want to do something and we won't give them a chance."

The other Board members began to argue amongst themselves.

Mr. Winstead tried to regain order by pounding his gavel. "Come to order! Come to order!" The Board members became quiet. "Now that's better. It's getting late and I think it might be best if we passed this matter on to the Music Committee. If there is no further business, I'll call this ..." Rev. Holtman timidly raised his hand. "Yes, Pastor, what is it?"

"Well, I'm not even sure I should concern you with this, but it's disturbing me," said Rev. Holtman. "The other day when I was going through my mail, I came across this envelope. I opened it up, and inside were these tickets - 253 tickets!"

"To a Sunday football game, eh Reverend?" laughed Mr. Roundbottom.

 "Well, it isn't that kind of ticket, Mr. Roundbottom. I feel silly saying this, but they simply have on them: **Admit One to Heaven, December 25th**."

"Oh, Bill, it's late!" sighed Mr. Winstead. "It surely must be some kind of sales gimmick."

"Yeah, that's what I thought, until I held them in my hand. And then I got the strangest feeling, like nothing I had ever experienced before."

"Here. Let me see!" Mr. Roundbottom reached across the table and grabbed the tickets away from Rev. Holtman. After Mr. Roundbottom examined them, they were passed around to the other members. As each person held them, they experienced the same feeling as did Rev. Holtman. For the first time, all the members of the board were smiling. It was unanimous, again a first. They decided that these tickets were no sales gimmick.

"I'd like to make a motion," said Mr. Roundbottom. "I move we call a special Church Council so that these tickets may be distributed in an equitable manner."

Seconds were heard from all over the room. The meeting was adjourned and everyone ran for the doors, eager to spread the word about the tickets.

Sigmund and Mortimer stood all by themselves in the Boardroom. "Well, it seems as though they got the message," said Mortimer. "But I don't think they realize that it isn't going to be that easy."

"Yeah, I agree, Mortimer. I don't think they realize that they have more than 253 people in this church. I wonder if the front office knew that they only sent down 253 tickets to a church that has ... well, they must have more than 600 members. Do you think we should phone upstairs?"

"No, Sigmund, I don't think that would be a good idea. It's never a good idea to question the front office. We'll just have to stand by and see what happens."

Act III
The Church Council

A special Church Council to consider the matter of the tickets was called to order by the chairman, Mr. Winstead.

"This special session of the Church Council will come to order. And you all know, we have some important business to discuss tonight. Frankly, it's the strangest thing I've run across in my fifteen years as Church Moderator. As many of you know, Pastor Holtman received 253 tickets in the mail, marked **Admit One to Heaven, December 25th**. At first we thought it was just a sales gimmick but we all agreed we had better investigate the matter a little further. So as I was instructed, I appointed a special committee. And so, I would now like to call on Mr. Jones for the investigating committee's report ... Mr. Jones."

"Thank you, Mr. Chairman. For the past two weeks we have made a thorough investigation of all such persons, operations or activities which bear the name HEAVEN. We ran the letters HEAVEN through my computer and got all the possible names which could come from those six little letters. We came up with four possibilities: a Harold Heavens across town, a Happy Heavens Smith from Ohio, and a Heavenly Health Foods Store. All said that they didn't know anything about any tickets. Our latest lead, the Peaceful Heaven Cemetery, said that they don't need to issue tickets ... people just drop in when they get ready. Therefore, Mr. Chairman, the report from the Special Investigating Committee is that the tickets appear to be legitimate!"

"Thank you, Mr. Jones. Are there any questions? No? Having none, we'll move on to the Deacons' report. As our spiritual leaders, we have asked the Deacons to advise the church on the authenticity of these tickets ... Mrs. Goodman?"

"Thank you, Mr. Chairman. We, the Board of Deacons, have been meeting over the past two weeks. We have argued the validity of these tickets over and over and it always comes down to the same thing. It's unScriptural, it's unfounded, it's unheard of, but when we hold them in our hands, we know they are for real." A buzz went throughout the meeting room. "Yes, Mr. Chairman, these tickets are from God and those who carry these tickets will be allowed to enter Heaven on December 25th."

A loud cheer went up from all those attending the Council meeting. "Come to order. Come to order!" cried Mr. Winstead. "We would now like to call upon our Pastor for anything he'd like to say ... Bill."

Rev. Holtman looked concerned as he slowly got to his feet. "If I was concerned when I *first* got these tickets, I'm even more concerned now."

"Don't worry, Bill, we'll give you one!" one of the Board members laughed and shouted out.

Rev. Holtman smiled. "John, that's exactly what concerns me. Who is going to get these tickets? We have 253 of them and we have a membership of 426 active members and 752 inactive members. Only 253 tickets for over 1,000 persons and who is going to decide who gets one and who doesn't?"

"Pastor," said John. "We may have over 1,000 names on the roll, but how many of them support this church with their time and money?" A few *"amens"* came from those present. "Sunday, Charles counted 173 people in worship. It seems simple to me. We are going to have a surplus."

"Well, I've thought about that but... well... let's take you as an example, John. Do you mind if I get personal?"

"No, Pastor. Go ahead," said John, smiling at the other Board members. "I have no skeletons to hide."

"John, there was a time when you never came to worship. I'd visit your home and I couldn't talk to you because the television drowned me out. Then when Judy became active in the youth group, you took an interest and before long you gave your life to the Lord and now you are one of the most capable trustees we have. If we had received these tickets then, you would have been left out. You see what I mean, John? What about the people who are now like you were then? Is it *fair?* I just don't know," Reverend Holtman said. John tightened his lips and nodded his head in agreement.

Reverend Holtman continued, "Mr. Chairman, I first of all think we should vote on whether to use these tickets at all, realizing that we might be incapable of giving them out fairly. And then, if we still decide to use them, an equitable system should be created for their distribution."

"Thank you, Pastor," said Mr. Winstead. "I agree. Wasting no more time, let's vote. All those in favor of using these tickets, raise your hand. Approved - 22. Opposed - None. Two abstaining. Who is that back there?"

"Little Tommy Jergenson," someone said.

"Tommy, what are you doing here?" asked Mr. Winstead. "Isn't Mary watching you in the nursery?"

"Oh, yes sir. But I asked her if I could come down and show you my friend, Eddie." A little boy came out from behind Tommy. "He moved in next door and he's coming to Sunday School with me Sunday. And I want you to meet him," said Tommy proudly.

"That's nice, Tommy," said Mr. Winstead. "Hello, Eddie. Now why don't you run along back to the nursery."

"Okay. Come along, Eddie. Good-bye."

"Kids! Here we are discussing such important matters and Tommy comes barging in here with that little dirty ... thing ... and interrupts us," complained Mr. Roundbottom.

"That little thing, for your information, lost his parents last year in an automobile accident and is a foster child," responded an angry Board member.

"Friends! Friends! Please!" said Mr. Winstead, "I know this is getting us all a bit irritable. I believe the vote was to use the tickets. Now I'll entertain a motion as to how they are to be distributed. Yes, Mr. Roundbottom?"

"I believe we should call a special Distribution Committee into session. I, for one, will be glad to serve."

"I bet you will," said Mr. Fleshman. "That's the only way you and your stuck-up wife will make it."

81

"I'll not stand for that!" complained Mr. Roundbottom. "Mr. Chairman, will you remind this person who paid for the gymnasium and who supports this church?"

"Gentlemen, gentlemen! Please! I think Mr. Roundbottom's suggestion is a good one. So that we don't have any screams of foul play later on, I suggest we take all the Board members' names and place them in a hat and the first nine drawn will be our committee." Everyone nodded their heads in agreement. "This committee will report to us by the first of next month. If there is no further business, I'll entertain a motion for adjournment."

"So moved. Meeting adjourned."

Act IV
Telephone Campaign

While the special Distribution Committee was busy deciding who would be the lucky 253 persons, a feeling of uncertainty fell upon the people of the First Church. Maybe a call to the Pastor might relieve a little of that uncertainty.

Buzz ... Buzz ... "Yes, Marsha?"

"Rev. Holtman, Miss Percy is on line one."

"Thank you. Yes, Miss Percy ... No, the committee has not determined what system will ... Yes, I'm sure they realize that the choir has been faithful ... Yes, I'm sure they need voices in Heaven ... What about the Musicale? Well, I thought it was all settled. No, the tickets aren't good until the 25th and the Musicale is the 24th ... I know you'll have a difficult time getting people together to practice ... I know they're saying they'd rather wait and sing up there... Well, I'm sure you can handle it ... Yes, you'll be informed of the meeting. Good-bye."

Buzz ... Buzz ... "Yes, Marsha?"

"Rev. Holtman, Mr. Roundbottom is on line two."

"Thank you, Marsha. Yes, Mr. Roundbottom ... Well, thank you. I've had quite a few favorable remarks on my sermon Sunday ... Yes, it was nice having people sitting in the aisles and that's why you're calling ... you want to talk about the idea of renovating the sanctuary. I thought you didn't think much of that idea. You were the one who wanted to relocate because of the neighborhood '*going to the dogs,*' to use your words ... Yes, I know we all have a right to change our minds. Well, to be frank, Mr. Roundbottom, a month ago this would have been good news. But now, well, it's a little too late ... Yes, I mean considering the tickets. Oh yes, the special Distribution Committee is working ... No, still no report ... I hope they will be ready by next week. Yes, it was good seeing your Uncle Fred on Sunday. I thought he was in Florida. I haven't seen him in worship for, I'd imagine eight years ... He's up for the winter? ... I thought you went to Florida for the winter! ... Oh, he wanted to talk to his lawyer about a will change seeing how he's so fond of the church ... Well, Mr. Roundbottom, I have a lot of things to do today. Yes, yes, I will inform you, Good-bye."

Buzz ... Buzz ... "Yes, Marsha?"

"Rev. Holtman, Mr. Winstead is on line one."

"Thank you, Marsha. I think I'm going to be out for the rest of the day. Hold all my other calls."

"Yes, Bob. Yeah, I'm surprised you got through ... Same at your place? Boy, this whole thing brings out the greedy side of people, doesn't it? ... Yeah, they've all called me too ... Yeah, the same thing. You know, Bob, I'm sorry this is happening. Those tickets ... I wish I'd been on vacation and they'd sat there on my desk unopened past the 25th. You know, I am seriously questioning the Lord's wisdom. Remember when the paper had the misprint and Bill's Barn had to face those stampeding people wanting those flat-screen televisions for $3.95? Yes, this goes against everything I've ever believed about the way the Lord moves. Oh sorry, Bob, I don't mean to unload on you ...

Thanks. Why are you calling? … Oh, they have finished their work. Well, we'll get the letter out today. See you then, Bob. Okay, good-bye."

Act V
The Report

For the first time in the history of the church, the Church Business Meeting was attended by a capacity crowd. People were sitting in the windows, and even standing in the doorways. The meeting was called to order with the pounding of the Chairman's gavel.

"This meeting will come to order," said Mr. Winstead. "Before we go on to the report I would like to say something. In all the years that I have been affiliated with this church, I have never been so disappointed in our conduct. Sure, we've had our differences and they have led to some pretty heated debates on occasion, but nothing like this with these tickets. Have we forgotten what church means? Has everything we've been taught and experienced over the years been for nothing? These tickets — are they so important that we would become greedy hypocrites in order to get one? I recall that we were warned about these tickets. And now, considering these last few weeks, I was wondering ..."

"Bob, we've already gone through this," interrupted a Board member. "Get on to the report!" Everyone began shouting, "The report! The report!"

"All right, all right," said Mr. Winstead. "If that's what you want. I now call on Phil Nebble to give us the report — Mr. Nebble."

"Thank you, Mr. Chairman and friends. First of all, I would like to say that being chosen to chair this committee was, indeed, the work from above, considering that I am an efficiency expert and quite capable in handling this sort of thing. I want to thank the committee for its tireless work. Some of us haven't had any sleep in the past few nights. I'm sorry that all the committee isn't here tonight. A few, I'm sorry to say, stayed home. They didn't make it. Well, on to the report."

"First of all let me share with you the way in which we arrived at the system for determining the selection of the ticket holders. Because we don't know what's in a person's heart we tried to stay away from one's religious qualifications. The only things we took into account were the visible things. So we listed attributes that we felt it would be necessary for a person to possess, and then assigned points based on that list of items. After we did this for every name given to us, and I might add that we had over 2,000 names to process, we tallied up the scores and the top 253 scores will be recommended by this committee to get a ticket."

Mr. Nebble then brought out a chart on which there were the headings: *Church Attendance, Financial Support, Special Gifts, Attendance at Meetings, Jobs in Church, Boards, Sunday School Teachers, Ushers.* "Now as you see on this chart, we have listed all the attributes that we consider our 'point items.' When all points were tallied up, the number of years that the person has been active in the church was used as a multiplier and that gave us our final total. Mr. Chairman, I have here the list of the top 253 scores." The people attending the Business Meeting began to stir and talk among themselves. There were groans of disappointment and shouts of joy as the list passed among the people. On this night there were more groans than shouts of joy.

"Come to order! Come to order, please!" shouted Mr. Winstead. "Thank you, Mr. Nebble. Are there questions about the 253 people who will get these tickets, or the report by Mr. Nebble and his committee ... yes, Connie?"

"Well, Mr. Winstead. My name isn't on here, and that's understandable since I have only been a member here for six months, but I am disturbed about the omission of Miss Dorsey." Everyone looked at the list and gasped when they could not find Miss Dorsey's name. "If there is anyone deserving a ticket, it certainly should be Miss Dorsey," continued Connie. "She is the person who led me and many others to the Lord through her sweet and patient witness." "Yes! Yes!" said the others

"In her way, she has done more for the church than anyone I know. Helen, you said yourself the other day that if Miss Dorsey wasn't in Heaven, you didn't want to go." Helen looked down in shame. Connie sat down, emotionally upset.

"Mr. Nebble," said Mr. Winstead. "Connie has a point. Would you care to speak to that?"

Mr. Nebble stood up. Looking serious, he said, "Let me point out again, that type of judgment can only be made by God. I may give someone ten points for patience, another may think it is worth eleven, or maybe eight. If we had taken into consideration things like faith, hope, and love, there would have been screams of outrage. So we stayed away from those things ..."

The discussion of the Business Meeting faded in the background and the two angels, Sigmund and Mortimer, began to walk to the exit shaking their heads.

"Well, Mortimer, if I may be allowed to say something without fear of being hit by lightning, the front office has really made a mess with this one. Why, this is the worst thing that could have happened to these people. Look at them! Faces twisted in anger, hands clenched in greed ... wanting to go to Heaven should inspire people to do good things, not this."

"Yes, I agree, Sigmund, but it isn't our job to criticize. We are merely to report. But I must agree with you. These tickets have turned them into a bunch of greedy people."

"I suppose the front office knows what it's doing. I'm sure they took into account everything that could go wrong down here. I just don't know, Mortimer, I just don't know. I suppose the risk that is being taken is worth it, but I sure could have thought of a better ..."

Sigmund was interrupted by a ball which bounced up into his arms. Two little boys came running after it. Mortimer reached down and handed the ball to its owner, little Tommy Jergenson. "Gee, thanks," Tommy said as he took the ball and ran off with his little friend, Eddie.

"It sure doesn't seem like they are affected by all this, does it, Sigmund?"

"No, it seems as though they are the only sane people around here! They are also the only ones who can see us."

Act VI
December 25th

The big day finally arrived, December 25th. At one minute past midnight they came: Roundbottom, Percy, Winstead, Nebble, the Jergenson family, Rev. Holtman, and all the rest. Their number: 253. They didn't know for sure how or where it would happen, but they thought the church building would be their best bet. So, for twenty long, squirming hours they sat in the sanctuary. No one dared move. It could happen in the twinkling of an eye.

At first, everyone tried to do the thing they thought would be the thing to do when entering Heaven. Some bowed their heads and prayed, some looked at the ceiling and grinned, some knelt, others raised their hands in praise. Still others said memory verses from the Bible (specifically learned for this occasion). Most, however, just looked around at their friends doing things they had never seen them do before. This lasted about an hour. Arms got tired, necks got stiff, memory verses ran out, and the children got hungry. No one had brought any food. Twenty hours of waiting. Imagine that with hungry, tired children.

Finally, one of the ticket holders stood up and said, "Look at us! Does this look like we are about to enter Heaven? It's Christmas! Let's sing a Christmas carol ... *Joy to the World,* that's it! Let's go to Heaven singing *Joy to the World!"*

Well, that got the troops stirred up and on their feet. However, after the fifteenth round of *Joy to the World* they began dropping like flies. On the twentieth attempt, only the children were singing.

"Hush!" said Miss Percy, and once again silence fell upon the room.

This was supposed to be a joyous occasion. Christmas! Soon everyone would be in Heaven! Guaranteed! What more could one want for Christmas? A ticket to Heaven! That's all they talked about, thought about. That's all they'd lived and fought for these past weeks, a ticket to Heaven! Now they each had one. They each had what they wanted more than anything else in all the world, and there they sat. Twenty-one hours of misery!

Twenty-one hours of thinking about what had happened in the past several weeks. Twenty-one hours of thinking about the lives they had lived. First on the list, 53rd on the list, 242nd on the list — it made no difference. They each held their ticket in their hand and thought of its price and the price they had paid for a lot of things in life. By worldly standards, they deserved a ticket to Heaven, but what about God's standards? And worst of all, was this the way Heaven was going to be? Gloomy people sitting around thinking such thoughts? Was this going to be their eternal Home?

It was now December 25th at 11:55 p.m. Just five more minutes and this day would end. Was God making fools out of them? No, they had already done that themselves. Was this some kind of practical joke after all? Perhaps it really was a sales gimmick. No, they held the tickets and knew they were from God, and they believed that in the next five minutes they would enter Heaven. The time had finally come. They all fixed their eyes on the Sanctuary clock. They leaned forward in their pews. Four minutes. Three minutes. Suddenly, down the center aisle came a figure. A long and eerie shadow ran before it.

"It's time! It's time!" shouted a few hysterical ticket holders.

"I'm going to *faint!*" said Miss Percy as she slumped back into her seat.

"Praise God! Oh, Lord, take me!" shouted some others.

Soon the shouting was over and the people were silent. Nothing had happened. The figure that had walked down the aisle was now standing before them ... little Tommy Jergenson!

"What's he doing here?" yelled an upset ticket holder.

"Scaring us like that!" gasped Miss Percy as she straightened her dress and hat.

Little Tommy tugged on Rev. Holtman's sleeve. "Tommy!" said Rev. Holtman. "You better go back to your seat! There is only a minute left."

"It can't wait," said Tommy.

"All right, what is it?"

"Rev. Holtman," said Tommy, "I want to give my ticket to my friend, Eddie."

As his words carried throughout the sanctuary, the other ticket holders gasped in disbelief. "Where are his parents?" they screamed. "Does he know what he's saying?"

"You see, Rev. Holtman," continued little Tommy, "I want

Eddie to have my ticket so he can be with his mommy and daddy in Heaven. Can I give him my ticket?"

The clock in the sanctuary struck midnight and one-by-one the people stood on their feet after hearing little Tommy's request. One-by-one they looked at their tickets and thought about what Tommy had just said. Everyone was quiet. One-by-one all 253 ticket holders pondered within their hearts the true meaning of Christmas. Heaven was within each of them all along. They didn't have to die to get there. They entered it the moment they brought Jesus into their lives.

When the church chimes struck twelve, the Christmas spirit entered the lives of those people in a mighty way. A lady in the back began to sing, then someone up front, then someone over to the side. Soon everyone in the sanctuary was singing as they had never sung before, *Joy to the World, the Lord Has Come.*

Rev. Holtman stood up and said, "Yes, Tommy. You may give your ticket to little Eddie. And we shall do likewise."

With that a loud "Hurrah" went up from the people. They left the sanctuary, hugging and kissing and singing and laughing. They ran into the streets of Commonsville, USA and they, too, began giving their tickets away to the people who were looking in from the outside to see what would happen. As quickly as it had filled up, the sanctuary was emptied.

In all of the excitement little Eddie was left behind in the back of the church. Alone again, he began to cry.

"Don't cry," said a voice from the shadows. "Come here,

Eddie. Don't be afraid."

Little Eddie walked slowly toward the shadow as he wiped the tears from his eyes. Eddie stepped back as the person stepped into the light. "Mr. Roundbottom!" Eddie said with a measure of fear in his voice.

"Yes, Eddie, it's Mr. Roundbottom." Kneeling down, he continued, "You know, Eddie, I never had any children. And I've got a big house that gets awfully lonely. Eddie, do you think you could come and live with me and Mrs. Roundbottom? I don't know much about raising little boys, but ..." Before Mr. Roundbottom could finish, little Eddie put his arms around Mr. Roundbottom's neck and gave him a big hug.

"Eddie," said Mr. Roundbottom, "I want to give you my ticket." Mr. Roundbottom then took Eddie home and it is said that no man was ever a better father.

Mortimer and Sigmund stood by, wiping tears of joy from their eyes. "It took a child, didn't it, Sigmund?"

"Yes, it did, Mortimer. Heaven is not something you get. It's something you give away. Just as God gave to the world His Son, Jesus. Heaven did come to this place tonight, and I'm glad that we were here."

"Yeah, the front office really knew what it was doing. I've enjoyed this visit to Mother Earth. Well, I suppose it's back to work we go."

"Yeah," said Mortimer. "To those blasted computers! I tell you, Sigmund, when we get back there, there are going to be some changes made ..."

About the Author

Reverend Wendell Mettey grew up in Cincinnati, OH. After obtaining a Bachelor's Degree in Economics from the University of Cincinnati, he spent several years as a social worker.

When he felt God calling him to the ministry, he enrolled at Southern Baptist Theological Seminary where he earned a Master of Divinity Degree (M.D.I.V.). Reverend Mettey has served as Pastor for several churches in the Cincinnati area. In 1991, after visiting war-torn Nicaragua and witnessing the poverty and devastation, he felt called by God to resign from his church and begin Matthew 25: Ministries.

Matthew 25: Ministries, a top-ranked international humanitarian aid and disaster relief organization, rescues and reuses 14,000,000 pounds of excess corporate products each year and redistributes them to people in need throughout the US and the world. Matthew 25: Ministries celebrated twenty years of service and the shipment of their 100,000,000th pound of aid in 2011.

Reverend Mettey and his wife Mickey (Michelle) have three children; Tim, Clare and Aaron. They are also the proud grandparents of Ethan, Sidney, Olivia, Cora, Noel and Ashlyn.

Reverend Mettey is the author of numerous devotional & inspirational publications. These include "Are Not My People Worthy? The Story of Matthew 25: Ministries" (released in 2004); "What God Desires The Story of the Center for Humanitarian Aid and Disaster Relief" (released in the 2008); "On Which Side of the Road Do the Flowers Grow?" (released in 2009) and "Meet Those Who Met the Master" (released in 2012). In addition to these books, Reverend Mettey has published several compilations of stories, sermons and reflections.

In June of 2003, Reverend Mettey received the Jefferson Award for Outstanding Public Service from the American Institute for Public Service and the Jacqueline Kennedy Onassis Award for Outstanding Public Service Benefiting the Local Community.